Adapted by Mickie Matheis

SCHOLASTIC INC.

New York   Toronto   London   Auckland

Sydney   Mexico City   New Delhi   Hong Kong

ISBN 978-0-545-22543-4

Published by Scholastic Inc.
SCHOLASTIC and associated logos are trademarks and/or registered trademarks of Scholastic Inc.

12 11 10 9 8 7 6 5 4 3   10 11 12 13 14 15/0

Designed by Angela Jun
Printed in the U.S.A.   40
First printing, September 2010

Carly Shay and her friends, Sam Puckett and Freddie Benson, were filming their weekly Web show, *iCarly*. Carly told the viewers they had a surprise planned.

"It's one of the most popular things we do here at *iCarly*," Sam added.

"MESSIN' WITH LEWBERT!" Carly and Sam said together into the camera. Sam pressed a button on the sound-effects remote. Cheers filled the studio. Lewbert was the doorman in Carly's apartment building. He was mean and nasty and had a huge, gross wart on his face. It was fun to mess with him!

Freddie explained to the viewers how they had hidden a confetti-cannon in a muffin basket. He played a demo video to show what would happen.

In the video Carly's brother, Spencer, walked up to the basket. "Look, a muffin basket!" he said. "I'm sure there's nothing *unusual* about these muffins. I think I'll have one." He squeezed his eyes shut and carefully reached into the basket.

BLAM! Confetti exploded all over Spencer's face!

"I wasn't expecting *that*!" said Spencer. He spit confetti from his mouth. Then the video clicked off.

"And now it's time to mess with Lewbert!"
Carly said.

Freddie turned on the Lewbert Cam. This
was a special camera that spied on Lewbert. It
zoomed in on him sitting in the lobby. He was
cleaning his fingernails with a fork. Gross!

Carly called their friend Mark on a walkie-talkie. Mark brought the muffin basket into the lobby and placed it in front of Lewbert. Then he left.

"Wait! Who's this for?" Lewbert yelled. But Mark was already gone. Lewbert thought the muffins in the basket looked tasty. As he reached for one, Sam pressed a button on a special remote control.

Suddenly there was a huge explosion. Lewbert was knocked across the lobby floor! It looked like Lewbert was really hurt.

Carly, Sam, Freddie, and Spencer all ran downstairs. They found Lewbert lying flat on his back. Muffin chunks were everywhere! They felt awful — they hadn't meant to really hurt Lewbert.

Carly noticed that Lewbert's wart was missing. "Oh, man, we blew his wart off!" Freddie said.

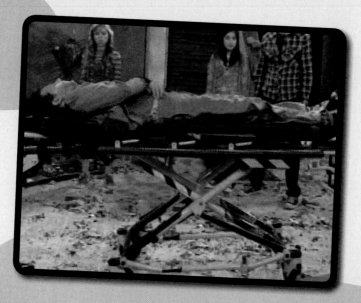

Just then an ambulance arrived. Lewbert was put on a stretcher. "Wait!" he shouted. "Where's my wart?"

Sam yelled and pointed to Carly's sneaker. Lewbert's wart was stuck to it! Eww! Carly screamed. Freddie quickly took off her shoe and gave it to the paramedics. Carly told them to just keep it. She was too grossed out to ever wear that shoe again!

The next day, Carly talked to the hospital and got some good news. Lewbert was going to be okay! "Well, not okay, but back to the way he was before," Carly told Sam and Freddie.

Spencer came into the room wearing Lewbert's doorman uniform. "I'm going to cover the front desk for Lewbert," Spencer said.

Lewbert had to stay in bed for at least a week. Spencer told Carly, Sam, and Freddie to check on Lewbert during the day. They didn't like the idea but agreed it was the right thing to do.

But they almost changed their minds when they saw his apartment. It was filthy! And Lewbert was still mean and nasty. He made them fluff his pillow, catch bugs to feed his lizard, and scratch his foot with a fork.

Meanwhile, Spencer was busy at the front desk. He had found Lewbert's CB radio and was using it to talk to truck drivers. Spencer called himself "The Doorman." He was telling jokes to two guys named Porkchop and Sledgehammer. They didn't like his jokes and told "The Doorman" to stay off the airwaves!

Spencer also got into a fight with a boy who lived in the building, named Chuck. Chuck was playing racquetball in the lobby. Spencer asked him to stop. But Chuck didn't listen. Chuck's father showed up and grounded him.

"I'll get you!" Chuck said as he shook his fist at Spencer.

Carly, Sam, and Freddie helped Lewbert again the next day. While the girls cleaned his apartment, Freddie installed a ceiling fan for him. But when Lewbert tried to turn on the fan, it crashed down on him and he was sent to the hospital again!

When Lewbert got home from the hospital
this time, Freddie's mom, Mrs. Benson, took
charge. "Why don't you kids run along?" she
suggested. "I'll look after Lewbert."

"Thank you, Mrs. Benson," Lewbert said.

"Please . . . call me Marissa," she told him.

"Marissa? That's a pretty name," Lewbert
said. Mrs. Benson giggled.

Carly, Sam, and Freddie looked at each other. Mrs. Benson never giggled. And Lewbert was never nice! It was weird.

Since Mrs. Benson was going to stay with Lewbert, Sam immediately left. Carly and Freddie thought they should stay and help. But then Lewbert asked Mrs. Benson to shave his back.

Carly and Freddie decided it was a good time to leave after all!

Mrs. Benson began spending a lot of time with Lewbert. This gave Freddie the freedom to do things his mother didn't like. One day he went to school without a belt. And he wore open-toed shoes.

"Wow, you're an animal!" Sam teased him.

"Doesn't it bug you that your mom and Lewbert are almost dating?" Carly asked Freddie.

"They're not dating. She's just being a good nurse," Freddie replied.

But it made him wonder. *Were* they dating? Would they get married? That meant Lewbert might be his stepfather! He couldn't let that happen.

Back in the lobby, Spencer was still telling jokes on the CB radio. "Hey, Porkchop and Sledgehammer, if you guys got married, would your last name be Sledgechop or Porkhammer?" he asked.

This really made the truckers mad! They wanted to know where The Doorman was. Spencer wouldn't tell them. But he didn't know that Chuck was listening. When Spencer went into another room, Chuck grabbed the CB radio. He told the truckers where they could find The Doorman.

After school, Freddie went to Lewbert's apartment. He quietly opened the door and peeked inside. His mother and Lewbert were having a candlelit dinner to celebrate Lewbert's recovery. He was going back to work the next day. Mrs. Benson had made a yummy fish loaf.

Lewbert was saying nice things about the meal. Then he said something nice to Mrs. Benson. "I'm looking at something pretty sweet," he said with a smile.

"Oh, Lewb!" Mrs. Benson giggled.

They touched their glasses together. "To us!" Lewbert said.

Freddie ran to find Carly and Sam. "You were right! My mom likes Lewbert! AAARRGH!" Freddie shouted. He was very upset. Carly and Sam tried to calm him down.

"We can fix this," Sam said. They began to think of a plan.

"What's the most important thing in the world to your mom?" Carly asked Freddie.

"I don't know — soap?" Freddie guessed. He was not in the mood to play games.

"You!" Carly said.

"You're her whole world," Sam added.

Carly told Freddie that if he got hurt, Mrs. Benson would want to take care of him. And she would forget about Lewbert. As crazy as it sounded, Freddie decided the plan was worth a try.

Lewbert and Mrs. Benson were in the lobby on their way out to dinner. But first, Mrs. Benson needed to rub some cream on Lewbert's wart. Just then Freddie's voice came from the stairwell.

"Mom, are you down there?" he called. Suddenly there was a crash! Freddie tumbled down the stairs into the lobby.

"Oh, my baby! Are you all right?" Mrs. Benson rushed to Freddie's side.

Don't get any blood on my floor!" Lewbert shouted.

"My son is hurt!" Mrs. Benson yelled.

"We don't have time for this!" Lewbert complained. He had made reservations at a fancy restaurant. And he really wanted cream on his wart.

"You'll just have to go without me!" Mrs. Benson told him. "My baby needs me!"

Carly and Sam came running. "What happened?" they asked.

Mrs. Benson told them Freddie fell down the stairs. "Probably because of these open-toed shoes," she said.

"WHAT ABOUT ME?" Lewbert wailed.

Mrs. Benson called Lewbert a mean, nasty man. Then she led Freddie away.

Who's going to rub cream on my wart?"
Lewbert whined.

He turned to Carly and Sam. "Would either
of you girls . . ." he began to ask.

"Ewww!" said Carly.

"Gross!" replied Sam.

Lewbert limped to his desk. The front door opened with a bang. Two big truckers walked in.

"Who are you clowns?" Lewbert asked rudely.

"Porkchop," said the shorter man. He looked mad.

"Are you The Doorman?" asked the taller man. He sounded mad.

"Yeah, I'm the doorman. Why?" Lewbert asked.

The two truckers came behind the desk and grabbed him.

Now it was their turn to mess with Lewbert!